Merry Christmas
2020

Love you,
Nana Carol
&
Papa Mike

D1404047

Based on the TV series *Dora the Explorer* as seen on Nick Jr.

SIMON AND SCHUSTER

First published in Great Britain in 2009 by Simon & Schuster UK Ltd
1st Floor, 222 Gray's Inn Road, London WC1X 8HB
A CBS Company

Originally published in the USA in 2009 by Simon Spotlight,
an imprint of Simon & Schuster Children's Division, New York.

A CIP catalogue record for this book is available from the British Library

ISBN 978-1-84738-673-1
Printed in China

10 9 8 7 6 5 4 3 2

Visit our websites: www.simonandschuster.co.uk
www.nickjr.co.uk

adapted by Christine Ricci
based on the screenplay "Dora's Christmas Carol Adventure" written by Chris Gifford
illustrated by Robert Roper

SIMON AND SCHUSTER/NICKELODEON

¡Hola! Soy Dora. It's my favourite night of the year. It's *Nochebuena!* That's what I call our Christmas Eve party. The tree is decorated, the picnic tables are full of treats, and all of the presents are under the tree. Everyone in the forest is so excited!

Hey! I can see a reindeer sneaking around the Christmas tree. I don't think that's just a reindeer. Who's under that reindeer mask? It's Swiper! Swiper is climbing up the Christmas tree. He's going to swipe the star. Oh, no! If Swiper swipes on Christmas, he'll get on Santa's naughty list!

I can hear bells ringing! Can you see anyone in the sky? It's Santa! Look! Santa is using his magic Christmas sparkles to stop Swiper. Santa is saving the party!

Santa has put Swiper on the naughty list for trying to swipe the Christmas tree star. To get off the naughty list, Swiper has to travel through time to Christmas in the past, when he was a baby, and to Christmas in the future, when he's older, so he can learn the true spirit of Christmas. We've got to help Swiper! Let's go! *¡Vámonos!*

The Grumpy Old Troll can help us travel through time. But first we have to answer his riddle. Do you know who has a white beard, rides in a sleigh, says "ho, ho, ho," and delivers gifts on Christmas eve? Santa! We solved the Grumpy Old Troll's riddle and he's giving us capes so we can travel through time.

To travel through time we have to shake our travel capes!

We're in the Christmas Forest of the Past. I can see a group of babies! Can you guess who the babies are? They are Isa, Tico, Boots, Benny, and even Baby Swiper. Oh, no! Baby Swiper swiped all of the other babies' Christmas presents.

Swiper feels bad that Baby Swiper made all of the babies cry. He's going to return the presents to the babies. I think Swiper is starting to learn the spirit of Christmas.

We travelled through time again, and now we're all little kids. Everyone was playing with their new Christmas toys when Little Kid Swiper swiped all the presents and tossed them into the forest.

Let's help Swiper find all of the toys that Little Kid Swiper swiped. Can you see a toy car for Benny, a bongo drum for Isa, a baseball mitt for Boots, a tricycle for Tico, and a rocking horse for me?

Thanks for helping Swiper find the presents. Swiper's getting the Christmas spirit!

Now we're in the Christmas Forest of the Future, when we're much older. Hey! Can you see an older Dora? Yeah, she's looking at the pine tree, but the tree doesn't have any Christmas decorations on it. Older Swiper swiped everything, and in the future, there won't be a Christmas Eve party at all.

We've got to help Swiper learn the true spirit of Christmas so he won't grow up to be like Older Swiper!

Oh, no! Older Swiper just swiped something else. He took Swiper's travel cape. Without the cape, Swiper can't travel back home!

Luckily, I know some friends who can help! Can you see Older Boots, Benny, Isa, and Tico? They want to help us get the cape back.

We've got to find Older Swiper, but we don't know where he went. Who do we ask for help when we don't know which way to go? Map! Map says that the wrapping-paper trail leads to the castle where Older Swiper lives. Can you see the wrapping-paper trail? Let's go!

We made it to the castle. Can you see Older Swiper? Yeah! He's asleep in his rocking chair. Older Swiper looks lonely. Swiper doesn't want to end up all alone on Christmas without any friends. He really wants to learn the true spirit of Christmas.

We need to find the purple travelling cape so Swiper can get home. Look around the castle. Can you see the purple travelling cape? You found it! Let's travel back home. *¡Vámonos!*

Z-Z-Z-Z-Z-Z

We made it home just in time for Santa to deliver our Christmas presents. Santa has presents for everyone except Swiper. He is still on the naughty list.

Instead of getting presents, Swiper has something that he wants to give us. What is Swiper giving us? It's his bunny. Swiper is giving it to us to thank us for helping him today.

Bells are ringing! Swiper has learned the true spirit of Christmas: It is better to give than to receive . . . or to swipe!

Swiper is no longer on the naughty list! Santa gives Swiper a bag full of presents and Swiper is giving all of his presents away. We helped Swiper learn the true spirit of Christmas. We did it! *¡Feliz Navidad!* Merry Christmas!